SOLAR

POWER

by Julia Vogel

ENERGY LAB:
SOLAR POWER

CHERRY LAKE PUBLISHING • ANN ARBOR, MICHIGAN

CHERRY LAKE Publishing

Published in the United States of America
by Cherry Lake Publishing
Ann Arbor, Michigan
www.cherrylakepublishing.com

Printed in the United States of America
Corporate Graphics Inc.
January 2013
CLFA10

Consultants: Dr. Barry D. Bruce, Professor of Biochemistry, Cellular, and Molecular Biology and the Microbiology Departments, University of Tennessee at Knoxville; Marla Conn, reading/literacy specialist and educational consultant

Editorial direction:
Lauren Coss

Book design and illustration:
Christa Schneider

Photo credits: iStockphoto, cover, 1; Shutterstock Images, Design Element (all), 5, 8, 12, 15, 17, 24; Lazar Mahai-Bogdan/Shutterstock Images, 6; Matt Jeppson/Shutterstock Images, 10; Tom Grundy/Shutterstock Images, 18; Ben Jeayes/Shutterstock Images, 21; Elena Elisseeva/Shutterstock Images, 27

Library of Congress Cataloging-in-Publication Data
Vogel, Julia.
  Solar power / Julia Vogel.
     pages cm. – (Energy lab)
  Audience: 8-9.
  Includes index.
  ISBN 978-1-61080-898-9 (hardback : alk. paper) – ISBN 978-1-61080-923-8 (paperback : alk. paper) – ISBN 978-1-61080-948-1 (ebook) – ISBN 978-1-61080-973-3 (hosted ebook)
1. Solar energy–Juvenile literature. I. Title.

  TJ810.3.V64 2013
  333.792'3–dc23

                              2012030464

Cherry Lake Publishing would like to acknowledge the work of The Partnership for 21st Century Skills. Please visit www.21stCenturySkills.org for more information.

TABLE OF CONTENTS

You are being given a mission. The facts in What You Know will help you accomplish it. Remember the clues from What You Know while you are reading the story. The clues and the story will help you answer the questions at the end of the book. Have fun on this adventure!

Your mission is to explore how energy from the sun can be put to work on Earth. How can sunshine light homes, heat water, and be turned into electricity? What technologies can help us use more solar power? Can sunshine replace other energy sources that are polluting the planet? How will solar power help shape our energy future? Check the facts in What You Know, then begin your mission to learn just how powerful solar energy can be.

WHAT YOU KNOW

★ Right now, more than 80 percent of the energy that powers our modern lifestyle comes from oil, coal, and natural gas. These are all **fossil fuels**.

★ Scientists want to produce energy in ways that are more efficient, less expensive, and better for the environment than our present energy sources.

★ Sunshine, or solar energy, is currently used to light homes, heat water, and produce electricity.

The sun might play an important role in meeting our future energy needs.

★ Energy from the sun comes to Earth in the form of **solar radiation**.

Jared O'Neil wants to know more about solar power. He plans to spend the next few weeks interviewing scientists and others who can help him learn more about solar energy and the work it can do. Your mission starts when you open Jared's journal.

I know the sun is a powerful star. Solar energy helps plants grow and powers the wind and the rain. Without the sun's energy, our planet would be just another lifeless rock in space. Today I'm visiting a university in Nebraska. Professor Tara Anderson is a solar astronomer who works there. She has agreed to show me the sun through the university's special telescope. First she tells me I should never ever look at the sun on my own. Doing that can cause serious damage to my eyes.

The sun is the closest star to Earth. It has been active for more than 4.5 billion years.

Through the telescope, the sun looks just like the huge ball of hot gas that it is. Professor Anderson explains that the sun is huge. It's so big that more than 1 million Earths could fit inside of it. The sun's energy comes from nuclear explosions deep inside it. "The sun's core is about 27 million degrees Fahrenheit, or 15 million degrees Celsius," says Professor Anderson. All that energy eventually heads out into space in electromagnetic waves. Most of the solar radiation reaching the earth is in the form of visible light. It comes in all the colors of the rainbow.

She tells me that green plants have a light-absorbing substance called chlorophyll. The energy that chlorophyll absorbs powers a chemical reaction between water and **carbon dioxide**. That reaction is called **photosynthesis**, and it's how green plants make energy. Photosynthesis makes **carbon**-based sugars. Plants and the animals that eat the plants depend on these sugars to live.

"You probably know that most of the energy we use today comes from fossil fuels," Professor Anderson says. "Fossil fuels come from animals and plants that died long ago. Over a very long time, they became buried deep underground. Heat and pressure from the rocks above them turned their remains into rich energy sources.

Without the sun, plants would not be able to make energy to survive.

We can burn these remains to run factories, heat homes, and power computers."

Professor Anderson says that demand for fossil fuels is growing as the earth's human population grows. More people use more energy.

"Fossil fuels aren't like sunshine, either," Professor Anderson says. "They are **nonrenewable** resources. That means Earth has only so much oil, coal, and natural gas.

Once they're used up, they're gone. That's why it's important to find a way to use alternative energy sources on a large scale. Solar power, wind, flowing water, and biofuels are major sources of alternative **renewable** energy."

As I leave the university, I think more about what Professor Anderson told me. If fossil fuels are really running out, we will need to find other ways to produce the energy they provide. I understand that plants and animals need the sun to survive. But I'm still not sure how the sun's energy could be used to light a dark room. ★

ARE YOU AN ALTERNATIVE ENERGY INNOVATOR?

You may already be using alternative energy in your daily life. Check your calculator, watch, and outside lights. Do they have solar cells? Next time you're with a parent or other adult who is getting gas, check the pump. Does the label say "10% ethanol"? That would mean one-tenth of the fuel comes from corn or other plants. Or the pump might read "20% biodiesel." Then your car may burn soybean or other plant oil—and smell like french fries!

"Ouch!" My hand just touched a rock baking in the hot desert sun. "Feels like a frying pan!" I am visiting Carlos Hernandez. He's a ranger at the Desert Pines State Park. The sun shines most of the time in the desert. I want to learn more about how people use sunlight for energy.

"Ancient American Indians used hot stones to heat water," Carlos tells me. "Stones have **thermal mass**, which means they can absorb heat and hold it. Today, we use thermal mass at the nature center to stay warm all winter."

Lizards are cold-blooded. They need sunlight to heat their bodies.

Carlos shows me around the nature center's patio. "See that lizard? He's absorbing sunlight too. He needs the sun's rays to keep his body warm." He tells me that some of the sun's radiation is reflected into our eyes in the form of light. This reflection allows us to see objects and colors. However, much of the sun's energy is absorbed as heat. People can use the sun's heat to warm water or heat buildings.

Ancient Pueblo American Indians built their houses using a mixture of stone or mud bricks called adobe. Adobe acts like the rock I touched. It bakes in the sun all day, holding heat. When the air cools, the adobe gives off heat energy into the air. It warms the building.

"We still use this style of heating today," Carlos tells me. "The nature center's walls are made of adobe."

He invites me inside the nature center. A wall of south-facing windows and skylights brighten the room we are in. "Clear glass lets the sun's radiation into the building," he explains. "Instead of paying for electric lamps, we have natural sunlight. This is called passive solar energy."

Carlos tells me that solar buildings in colder places use sunlight to heat tile floors or columns of water that store extra heat. These buildings may also have a

Adobe absorbs the sun's heat during the day and gives it off at night.

greenhouse, where glass traps so much solar heat that tropical plants can grow year-round.

"But if solar energy has been used for such a long time, why do we still use so many fossil fuels?" I ask.

"Not every building is designed like the nature center," Carlos explains. "Does your house have skylights and walls with thermal mass? It's difficult and expensive to add these things to existing buildings. These features won't work well in many places, such as a house in the northern woods."

Carlos also reminds me that passive solar energy can't power a lot of our electric devices, such as lights, computers, and refrigerators. "The sun radiates more energy to Earth in an hour than humans use in a year," he says. "But to turn this energy into something we can use, we have to transform it into electricity."

I thank Carlos for showing me around. I'm ready to learn more about how sunshine becomes electricity. ★

THE BEST THERMAL MASS

What's a good building material choice for passive solar buildings? With an adult's help, you can test different materials in your oven to find out. Collect five cans and fill each one halfway with one of five different materials: water, sand, small stones, salt, and soil. Put the cans in an oven heated to 150 degrees Fahrenheit (65°C). After one hour, carefully remove the cans from the oven using protective oven mitts. Take the temperature of each can every five minutes and record your findings. Which material cools the fastest? Which cools the slowest? Which material would be the best choice as a building material for a passive solar house?

Today, I've traveled to a research facility in Arizona. The facility is known for its use of solar power. I'm up on the roof with researcher Dr. Raj Stevens. The roof is covered with solar panels. I have seen solar panels from the ground before, but never this close up.

Dr. Stevens points out that each panel is made up of dozens of smaller squares, or solar cells. "That's where sunlight is transformed into electricity," he says. The cells are called PVs, or photovoltaic cells. "*Photo* means light," he tells me, "and *voltaic* means electricity."

The first PVs were built during the 1970s. "Those early cells were less than 1 percent efficient," says Dr. Stevens. "Imagine your homework was a set of math problems. If you were 100 percent efficient, you could finish in one hour. How long would it take if you were 1 percent efficient?"

Holy cow! One hundred hours! No wonder scientists kept working to try to create better PVs. During the 1950s, scientists found that they could use silicon, an element found in sand, to make a 4 percent efficient solar cell. By the 1960s, PVs connected into solar panels were

Photovoltaic solar panels capture energy from the sun and turn it into electricity.

efficient enough to power a research **satellite** orbiting the earth.

Dr. Stevens explains that wires coming from the panels can power lights and other building needs immediately. But they can also feed energy into a battery. This battery transforms electrical energy from the solar cells into chemical energy. Inside the battery, chemical

SOLAR POWER IN SPACE

Solar cells work even better in space than they do on Earth. In space, there are no clouds to block the sunshine. Scientists first used solar cells in space in 1958 on the satellite *Vanguard I*. This satellite, which was powered by six solar cells, collected data for six years to send back to Earth. Today, many kinds of satellites orbit the earth powered by solar cells. Even though there are no clouds in space, some of the solar energy these satellites collect is still stored in batteries. On the *International Space Station*, winglike solar arrays power operations, experiments, and life-support systems for a crew of six.

energy can be stored to use later. But Dr. Stevens says that batteries are expensive. And they can only store so much energy. These facts mean that most people using solar panels usually still have to use some energy from coal-powered plants.

"The panels work well for our science building, where we want to show people that clean, renewable energy is a possibility," Dr. Stevens says. "But the panels are still less than 20 percent efficient, and they cost a lot to install. Coal, which is the fuel used most often to generate electricity, is still more efficient."

People use a lot of energy to light buildings at night when the sky is dark.

"Doesn't the energy made by the solar panels mean you spend less money on electricity?" I ask.

"Yes, but PVs are so expensive," says Dr. Stevens. "It takes at least ten years of energy savings to pay back their cost."

Dr. Stevens has given me a lot to think about. Solar energy can work to power a single building. But it's not very efficient, and it can be very expensive. I wonder if there is a way for these solar panels to power more than just one building at a time. ★

I want to learn more about solar power on a large scale. I'm on my way to a farm in the California desert. From a distance, the crop looks like acres and acres of mirrors.

When I arrive, I meet with Veronica Lekander. Veronica is the farm's chief engineer. "I just visited a new PV solar plant in Israel," Veronica tells me. "It has 18,500 PV panels and produces 9 million kilowatt-hours of electricity per year." From science class, I remember that

At a solar farm, electricity can be mass-produced using the sun's energy.

a kilowatt-hour is a unit measuring how many kilowatts of power are used in an hour.

Veronica tells me her system is different. Instead of using solar light, her farm uses solar heat to create electricity. This is called concentrated solar power, or CSP. I remember the big windows at the nature center. The windows captured the sun's heat to warm the building. This solar farm traps heat in a similar way but uses it to create electricity.

We're close to the rows and rows of mirrors now. Each one is very long and shaped like an animal feed trough. Veronica points to the closest one. "See that tube down the middle?" she asks. "The tube is filled with oil. The curved mirrors catch the sunlight and focus it on the tubes. Sensors help the mirrors track the sun across the

EARLY CSP

Concentrated solar power has been around for a long time. During the 1830s, a British astronomer named John Herschel made a solar oven using an insulated box. Reflectors inside the box concentrated the sun's heat to cook food. Ever since then, inventors have been experimenting with ways to harness the sun's heat.

sky all day. The mirrors catch the sun's heat to heat up the oil. After the mirrors heat the oil, the oil heats water in the tubes to a boil. The water becomes steam. The steam turns a turbine. Then the turbine powers an electricity generator."

We drive past more and more rows of sun-collecting mirrors. "The CSP system works well, but like all energy options, it is imperfect," Veronica says. "One problem is how much land solar farms require. As you can see, the mirrors take up a lot of space. This land was once habitat for animals."

Veronica tells me territorial animals such as desert tortoises have the biggest problem with solar farms. These animals can't just move on to a new place when solar mirrors take over their habitat. Also, eagles, hawks, and other birds sometimes die when they crash into long solar transmission lines.

Another problem is cost. All the land and equipment to make electricity from solar energy is very expensive. Right now, solar power is about five times as expensive as electricity created by power plants that use fossil fuels.

"But remember," says Veronica, "engineers are improving the technology every year. As it gets more efficient, solar power plants will need less land. It will also cost less."

Producing solar energy on a large scale is expensive and takes up a lot of animal habitat.

Sunshine may be free, I think to myself, but solar power isn't cheap. I wonder how solar power works in places that aren't as sunny as a California desert. ★

I can see how solar energy would work well in a place famous for its sunny skies. But I wonder how it could work in a rainy place like Washington. I also wonder if solar power could ever replace gasoline as a fuel for cars.

I'm meeting with sixth-grade science teacher Michael Ali at his school in Glenwood, Washington. Today is the school's science fair.

"You picked a great day to visit, Jared!" Mr. Ali says. "My students have been studying solar power. Let's head out to the parking lot to take a look at what they've done."

He sees me looking doubtfully at the cloudy skies out the window. "Don't worry. Cloudy skies don't necessarily mean a place can't use solar power. Germany is a leader in solar power, and it gets even less sunshine than Glenwood. PV panels still work on cloudy days, just not as efficiently as they do on clear days."

Mr. Ali takes me to a student's presentation featuring a model PV panel. Wires from the solar panel lead to a large battery. I remember from the university that the electrical **current** from the solar panel charges the chemical solution inside the battery. This chemical energy is stored. It can be used later to make electricity.

"There's a real drawback to solar power around here," Mr. Ali says. "We need to be able to store a lot of energy for the really cloudy days. These big batteries take up tons of space. They also cost a lot of money."

Next, Mr. Ali leads me to a small racecourse set up in the parking lot. Eight solar-powered toy cars rush down the track. The students who built them cheer the cars on. The cars use solar batteries as their power source. The car that crosses the finish line first looks more like a wing on wheels than my family's car.

"Glenwood uses a lot of solar power," Mr. Ali says. "But even with our solar power, the town still uses as much

NEVER-ENDING SUNSHINE

One reason people like solar power is that the sun is reliable. The amount of energy reaching our atmosphere from the sun is almost constant. However, the amount of sunshine available for work is not constant. The amount of energy reaching a particular spot on Earth can vary due to the weather, the time of day, the time of year, and the area's geographic location. Because of the shape of the earth, the equator gets the most direct sunlight. The farther north or south a place is, the less energy it receives.

People sometimes race small solar-powered cars, but these cars look very different from regular cars.

oil as other towns. We haven't found a practical way to convert solar power into the kind of liquid fuel that powers today's cars."

He tells me about a solar car race in Australia. People drive cars nearly 1,900 miles (3,000 km) across the

Australian Outback to prove that solar energy can power cars. But with heavy panels and big batteries to carry, the technology isn't practical for everyday cars.

"PVs won't be powering our buses and trains anytime soon, either," Mr. Ali says. "But scientists have found ways to power other large vehicles using solar power." He points me to a presentation showing posters of solar boats, airplanes, and space vehicles.

"In 2007, a PV-powered boat crossed the Atlantic Ocean using only solar power," Mr. Ali says. "And the military has been testing solar-powered unmanned airplanes."

Mr. Ali reminds me that scientists are using the sun's energy to power objects far away from Earth as well. Approximately 44 percent less sunshine reaches Mars than Earth. But it was enough to power a solar-powered rover that explored the planet's surface for six years. A bit closer to home, Japanese scientists are working on an orbiting satellite that will beam enough solar energy back to Earth to power 294,000 homes.

Wow! Solar energy is more common than I thought. Although it has some major drawbacks, scientists are working hard to overcome these problems. I think solar energy might have an exciting role in our energy future! ★

Good work! You've learned a lot about solar power. You know that solar power can't solve all of our energy problems, but it can help. Photovoltaic solar panels on homes and businesses are one option, but they are inefficient. It can take many years for them to save enough electricity to be worth the cost of installing them. These PV solar panel systems can only provide solar power on a small scale. Big solar farms can provide solar power on a larger scale. However, these farms take up a lot of land, including former animal habitats. But researchers keep improving technologies. Soon, more and more of our energy can come from renewable resources like the sun. Shine on!

CONSIDER THIS

★ What parts of the world are especially rich in solar resources? Why?

★ What are some reasons people choose to not use solar power?

Do you think it's worth installing solar panels on your house?

- ★ How can solar power help protect wildlife and the natural environment?
- ★ How is concentrated solar power different from photovoltaic solar power?
- ★ What are some reasons people choose to use solar power?

carbon (KAHR-buhn) an element in living things that can trigger climate change in excess amounts

carbon dioxide (kahr-buhn dye-AHK-side) a gas released by the burning of fossil fuels

current (KUR-uhnt) in science, the flow of an electrical charge through a substance

fossil fuel (FAH-suhl fyoo-uhl) coal, oil, or natural gas formed from ancient plants and animals

nonrenewable (nahn-ri-NOO-uh-buhl) when something cannot be replaced once it is used up

photosynthesis (foh-toh-SIN-this-sis) a process through which carbon dioxide, water, and light energy are converted to energy for plants

renewable (ri-NOO-uh-buhl) when something can never be used up

satellite (SAT-uh-lite) an object that travels around another object

solar radiation (soh-lur ray-dee-AY-shuhn) energy given off by the sun

thermal mass (THUR-muhl mas) the property of a material that allows it to absorb, store, and release heat

BOOKS

Hansen, Amy S. *Solar Energy: Running On Sunshine*. New York: Rosen, 2010.

Kaye, Cathryn Berger. *A Kids' Guide to Climate Change & Global Warming: How to Take Action!* Minneapolis, MN: Free Spirit Publishing, 2009.

Richards, Julie. *Solar Energy*. Tarrytown, NY: Marshall Cavendish, 2009.

WEB SITES

Alliant Energy Kids

http://www.alliantenergykids.com/ energyandtheenvironment/renewableenergy/022400

Learn more about the history of solar power.

Energy Kids

http://www.eia.gov/kids/energy.cfm?page=solar_home-basics

This U.S. Energy Information Administration site provides maps of solar resources and more.

Kids and Energy

http://www.kids.esdb.bg/solar.html

Learn more about how the sun's heat gets turned into electricity.

BuILD A SOLAR OVEN

Save a small pizza box. Cut the lid on three sides to make a rectangular flap. Cover the inside of the flap with aluminum foil with the shiny side out. Next, seal the opening with strong plastic wrap, using tape to secure it firmly. Finally, line the inside of the box with sturdy black paper. Now you can cook s'mores in the afternoon sun! What does the aluminum foil do?

GREENHOUSE GLASS JARS

Place two identical thermometers side by side on a sunny table outside or on a shelf by an open window. After five minutes, record their temperatures. Then place a glass jar over one thermometer. Record each temperature every minute for ten minutes. Try the test again on another day with two jars, one lined with black construction paper and one lined with aluminum foil, shiny side out. Check the temperatures after ten minutes. What parts of our atmosphere act like the glass jar in your experiment, trapping heat? What absorbs heat? What reflects it?

ABOUT THE AUTHOR

Julia Vogel has written dozens of children's books about science and nature. She holds a doctorate in environmental studies and teaches environmental management to college students. When she isn't writing or teaching, she enjoys sunny hikes and shady picnics with her family and dog in Columbia, Maryland.

ABOUT THE CONSULTANTS

Barry D. Bruce is a Professor of Biochemistry, Cellular, and Molecular Biology and Chemical and Biomolecular Engineering at the University of Tennessee, Knoxville.

Marla Conn is a reading/literacy specialist and an educational consultant. Her specialized consulting work consists of assigning guided reading levels to trade books, writing and developing user guides and lesson plans, and correlating books to curriculum and national standards.